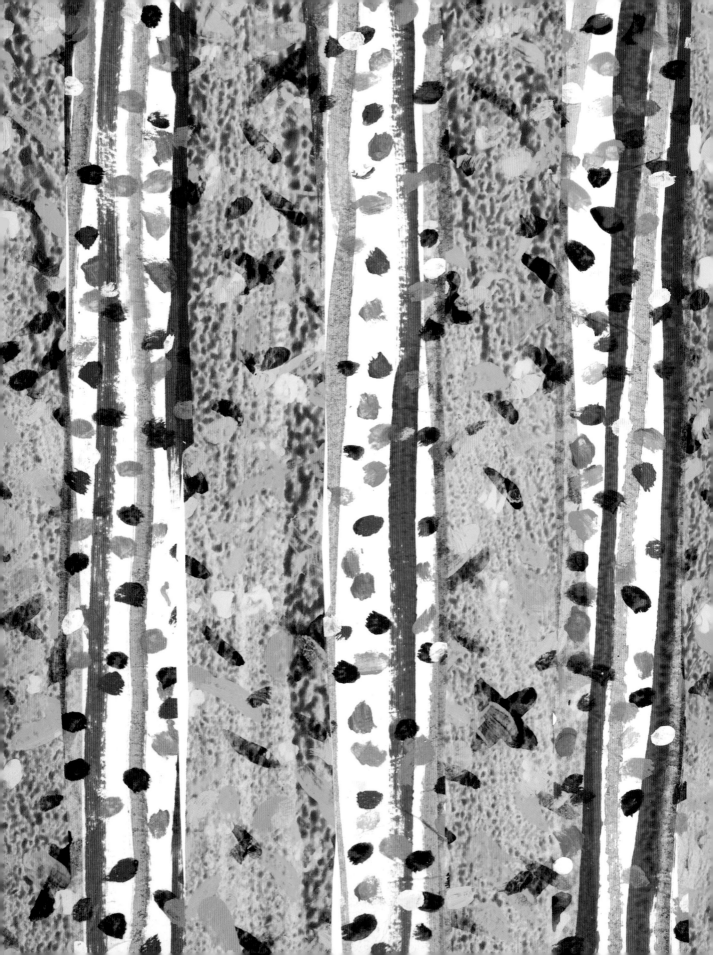

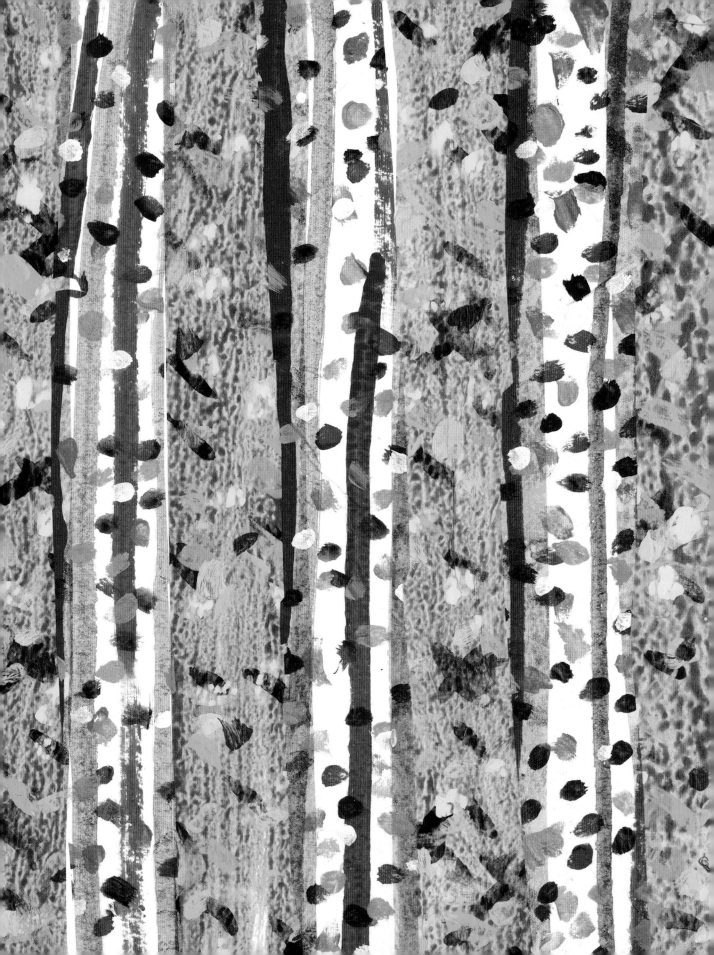

Author's Note

North America is filled with thousands of species of wildlife. These creatures have lived in their habitats for centuries. Together, we can work to ensure that they will remain wild and free forever. This book features ten of these great American animals.

The author wishes to thank Michael Sampson for his help in the preparation of this text.

For more information about Eric Carle or his books, please visit eric-carle.com
The Eric Carle Museum of Picture Book Art was built to celebrate the art that we are first exposed to as children. Located in Amherst, Massachusetts, in the United States of America, the 40,000-square-foot museum is devoted to national and international picture book art. Visit carlemuseum.org

PUFFIN BOOKS

Published by the Penguin Group
Penguin Books Ltd, 80 Strand, London WC2R 0RL, England
Penguin Group (USA) Inc., 375 Hudson Street, New York, New York 10014, USA
Penguin Group (Canada), 90 Eglinton Avenue East, Suite 700, Toronto, Ontario, Canada M4P 2Y3 (a division of Pearson Penguin Canada Inc.)
Penguin Ireland, 25 St Stephen's Green, Dublin 2, Ireland (a division of Penguin Books Ltd)
Penguin Group (Australia), 250 Camberwell Road, Camberwell, Victoria 3124, Australia
(a division of Pearson Australia Group Pty Ltd)
Penguin Books India Pvt Ltd, 11 Community Centre, Panchsheel Park, New Delhi – 110 017, India
Penguin Group (NZ), 67 Apollo Drive, Rosedale, North Shore 0632, New Zealand
(a division of Pearson New Zealand Ltd)
Penguin Books (South Africa) (Pty) Ltd, 24 Sturdee Avenue, Rosebank, Johannesburg 2196, South Africa

Penguin Books Ltd, Registered Offices: 80 Strand, London WC2R 0RL, England

puffinbooks.com

First published in the USA by Henry Holt and Company, LLC, 2007
Published in Great Britain in Puffin Books 2007
Published in this edition 2009
10 9 8 7 6 5 4 3 2 1

Text copyright © the Estate of Bill Martin Jr, 2007
Illustrations copyright © Eric Carle, 2007

The moral right of the author and illustrator has been asserted

Made and printed in China
All rights reserved

British Library Cataloguing in Publication Data
A CIP catalogue record for this book is available from the British Library

ISBN: 978–0–141–38445–0

Baby Bear, Baby Bear, What Do You See?

By Bill Martin Jr
Pictures by Eric Carle

PUFFIN

Baby Bear,
Baby Bear,
what do you see?

I see a red fox
slipping by me.

Red Fox,
Red Fox,
what do you see?

I see a flying squirrel
gliding by me.

Flying Squirrel,
Flying Squirrel,
what do you see?

I see a mountain goat
climbing near me.

Mountain Goat,
Mountain Goat,
what do you see?

I see a blue heron
flying by me.

Blue Heron,
Blue Heron,
what do you see?

I see a prairie dog
digging by me.

Prairie Dog,
Prairie Dog,
what do you see?

I see a striped skunk
strutting by me.

Striped Skunk,
Striped Skunk,
what do you see?

I see a mule deer
running by me.

Mule Deer,
Mule Deer,
what do you see?

I see a rattlesnake
sliding by me.

Rattlesnake,
Rattlesnake,
what do you see?

I see a screech owl
hooting at me.

Screech Owl,
Screech Owl,
what do you see?

I see a mama bear
looking at me.

Mama Bear,
Mama Bear,
what do you see?

I see . . .

a red fox,

a flying squirrel,

a prairie dog,

a striped skunk,

a screech owl and . . .

a mountain goat,

a blue heron,

a mule deer,

a rattlesnake,

**my baby bear
looking at me –
that's what I see!**

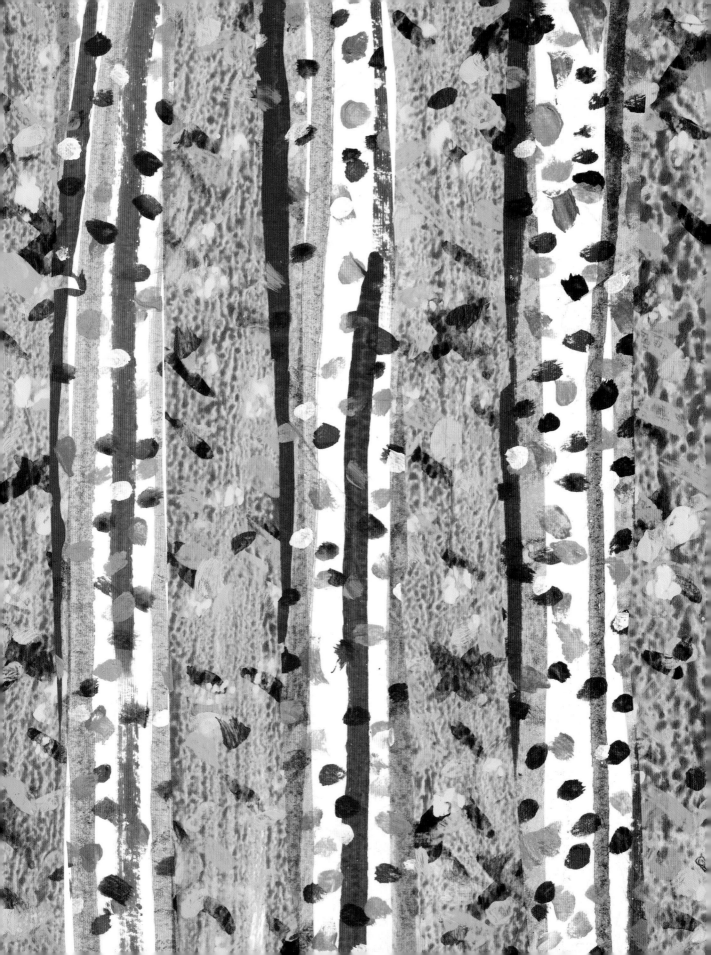

Other titles in the series

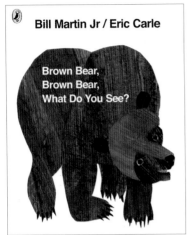

Paperback
ISBN: 978–0–141–50159–8

Paperback
ISBN: 978–0–140–54519–7

Paperback
ISBN: 978–0–141–50145–1

Also by Eric Carle

Paperback
ISBN: 978–0–140–56932–2

Sticker book
ISBN: 978–0–141–50196–3

Board book slipcase
ISBN: 978–0–141–38511–2

Novelty hardback
ISBN: 978–0–141–38506–8

Paperback
ISBN: 978–0–140–50398–2

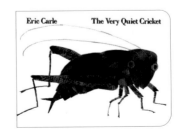

Board book
ISBN: 978–0–241–13785–7

Board book
ISBN: 978–0–241–13590–7